WHAT DOES A QUARTERBACK DO?

Paul Challen

PowerKiDS press™

New York

Published in 2015 by The Rosen Publishing Group, Inc.
29 East 21st Street, New York, NY 10010

Produced for Rosen by BlueApple*Works* Inc.
Art Director: Tibor Choleva
Designer: Joshua Avramson
Photo Research: Jane Reid
Editor for BlueApple*Works*: Melissa McClellan
US Editor: Joshua Shadowens

Photo Credits: Cover left, p. 7 Susan Leggett/Shutterstock; Cover right, p. 5, 8, 9, 20 James
Boardman/Dreamstime; p. 1, 10, 11, 12, 13, 14, 15, 16, 18, 21, 22, 23, 29 Andy Cruz; p. 3 Alhovik/
Shutterstock, background Bruno Ferrari/Shutterstock; p.4, 19 Aspen Photo/Shutterstock; p. 6,
24, 25 Richard Paul Kane/Shutterstock; p. 17 Mark Herreid/Shutterstock; p. 26 left, 27 bottom
Scott Anderson/Dreamstime; p. 26 right, 27 top Jerry Coli/Dreamstime; p. 28 Cynthia Farmer/
Shutterstock

Library of Congress Cataloging-in-Publication Data

Challen, Paul C. (Paul Clarence), 1967–
 What does a quarterback do? / by Paul Challen.
    p. cm. — (Football smarts)
Includes index.
ISBN 978-1-4777-6986-7 (library binding) — ISBN 978-1-4777-6987-4 (pbk.) —
ISBN 978-1-4777-6988-1 (6-pack)
1. Quarterbacking (Football)—Juvenile literature. I. Title.
GV951.3.C53 2015
796.33—dc23
                                    2013049388

Manufactured in the United States of America

CPSIA Compliance Information: Batch #WS14PK8 For Further Information contact: Rosen Publishing, New York, New York at 1-800-237-9932

TABLE OF CONTENTS

THE FOOTBALL TEAM

It takes a lot of people to make up a football team. A team is made up of an **offense** and a **defense**, both with very different jobs to do. In a pro game, players usually play either offense or defense, but not both. In youth football, it is common to play on both sides of the ball.

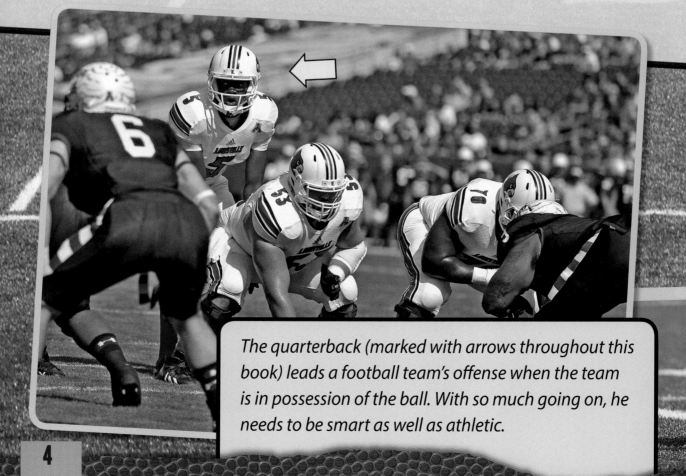

The quarterback (marked with arrows throughout this book) leads a football team's offense when the team is in possession of the ball. With so much going on, he needs to be smart as well as athletic.

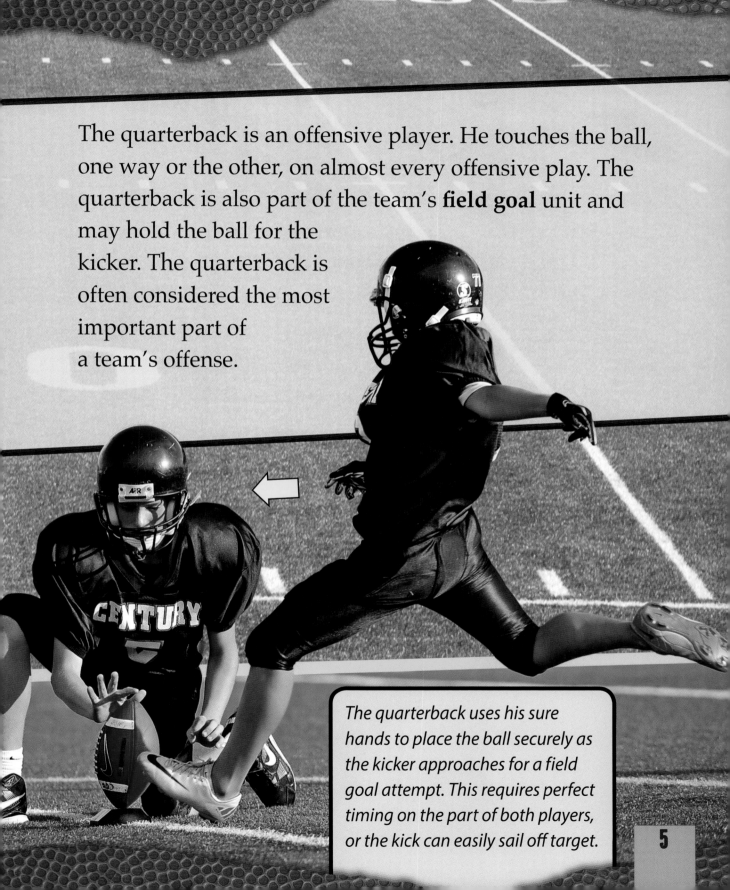

The quarterback is an offensive player. He touches the ball, one way or the other, on almost every offensive play. The quarterback is also part of the team's **field goal** unit and may hold the ball for the kicker. The quarterback is often considered the most important part of a team's offense.

The quarterback uses his sure hands to place the ball securely as the kicker approaches for a field goal attempt. This requires perfect timing on the part of both players, or the kick can easily sail off target.

QUARTERBACKS RULE!

The quarterback on a football team is the player in charge of the offense. To play this position, you have to be a great athlete, and you must understand the game very well. Quarterbacks must be strong and agile, and able to throw a football quickly and accurately.

Quarterbacks are not always big boys or men, but height and muscle are advantages. A quarterback who is tall enough to easily see over his blockers tends to throw with much more accuracy than one who can't.

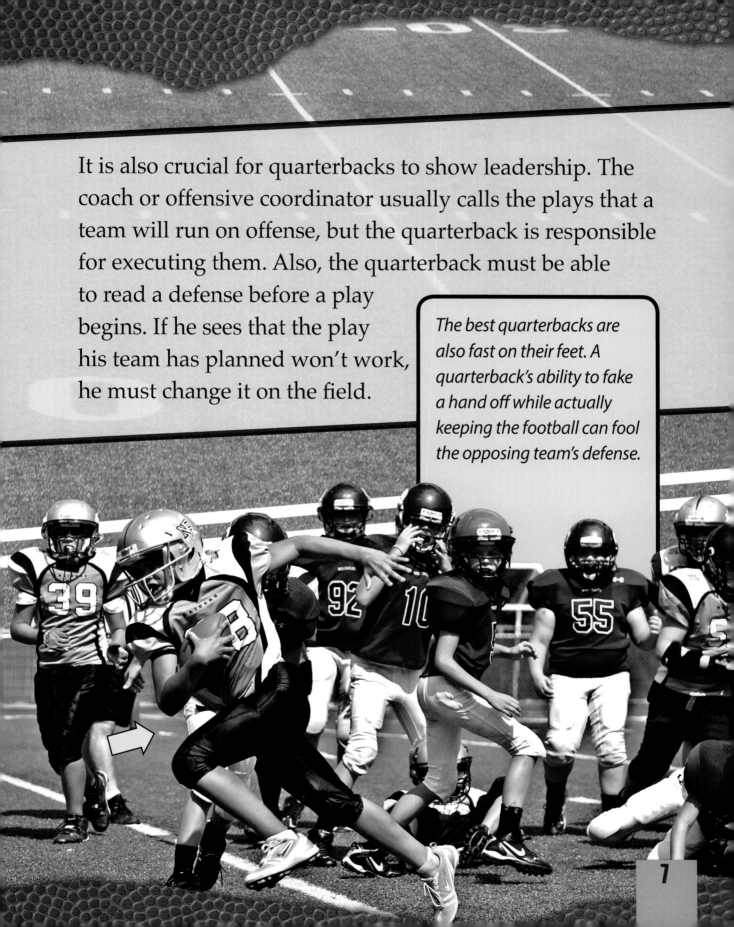

It is also crucial for quarterbacks to show leadership. The coach or offensive coordinator usually calls the plays that a team will run on offense, but the quarterback is responsible for executing them. Also, the quarterback must be able to read a defense before a play begins. If he sees that the play his team has planned won't work, he must change it on the field.

The best quarterbacks are also fast on their feet. A quarterback's ability to fake a hand off while actually keeping the football can fool the opposing team's defense.

STRATEGY

When a football team has the ball, the offense must move it down the field using running or passing plays and attempt to score a touchdown or kick a field goal. The defense tries to stop them. Both sides face off at the **line of scrimmage** on each play in a game.

The offensive line protects the quarterback when the ball is snapped. Receivers get ready to run their pass routes, and the running back prepares for a hand off behind the quarterback.

DID YOU KNOW?

One of the most exciting offensive plays is the quarterback option. On taking the snap, the quarterback sprints left or right, following his **blockers**. Depending on the position of the defensive players, the quarterback has the option of running forward to gain yards, passing the ball downfield to a receiver, or tossing the ball back to a running back.

Offensive players need skills like throwing, running, catching, and blocking. When an offense sets up to play, it usually features pass-catchers (receivers), players who run with the ball (running backs), and blockers (the offensive line). The quarterback stands behind an offensive lineman called the center, who snaps the ball through his legs to the quarterback to begin each play.

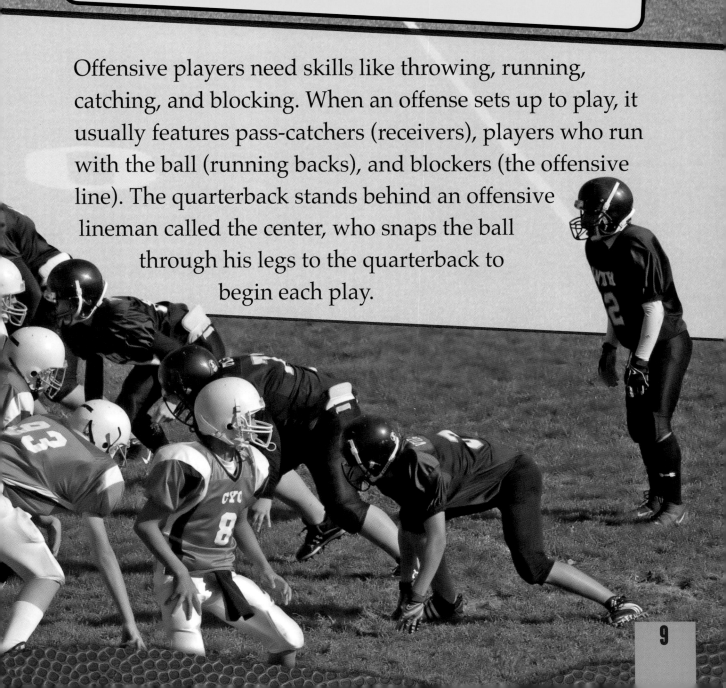

THE RIGHT STANCE

The quarterback needs to take a solid **stance** when receiving the snap. He balances himself by bending at the knees with his feet placed about shoulder width apart. The quarterback needs to make sure his hands are held firmly yet flexibly because if he grips too tight, he'll **fumble** the ball.

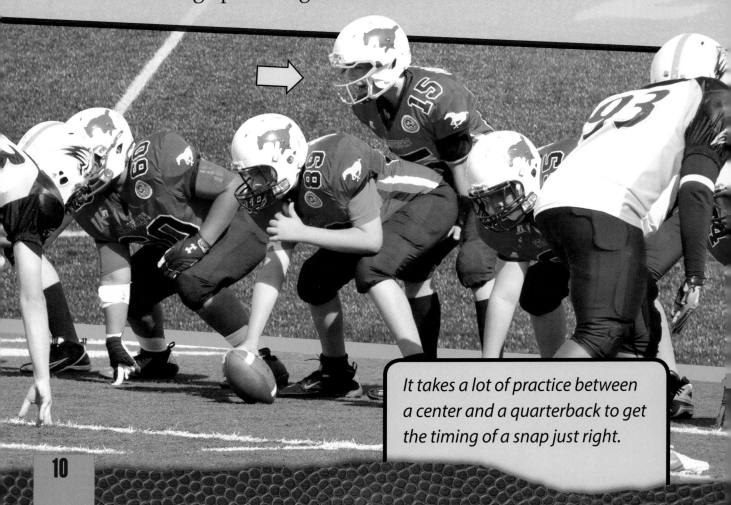

It takes a lot of practice between a center and a quarterback to get the timing of a snap just right.

A quarterback can receive a snap in two ways. He can stand right behind the center and get the ball directly from the center's hands, or he can stand a few yards behind the center, who will pass it between his legs and through the air. The **formation** a team uses for this longer snap is called the shotgun.

The shotgun formation gives a team a lot of offensive options, but it almost always results in a passing play. The quarterback has to be ready to receive the snap from the center and hit a receiver with an accurate pass.

RUN OR PASS

The quarterback can decide on two basic options for his team on offense: a running play or a passing play. Both of these are effective ways to gain yards and move a team down the field. Both plays require the whole team to be coordinated and for each player to carry out his assignment in running, blocking, and other ways.

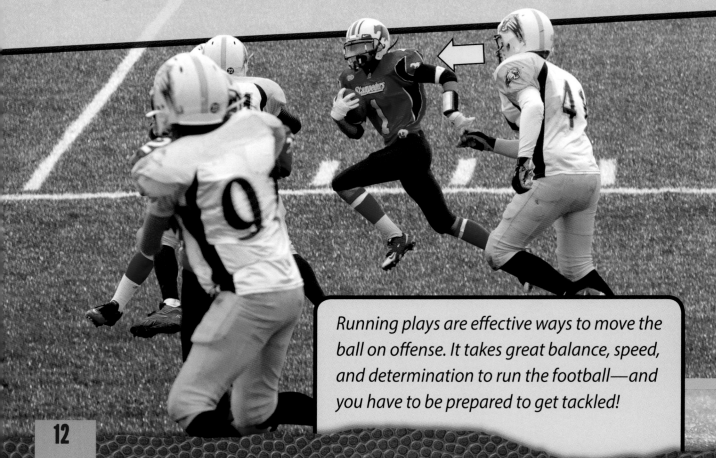

Running plays are effective ways to move the ball on offense. It takes great balance, speed, and determination to run the football—and you have to be prepared to get tackled!

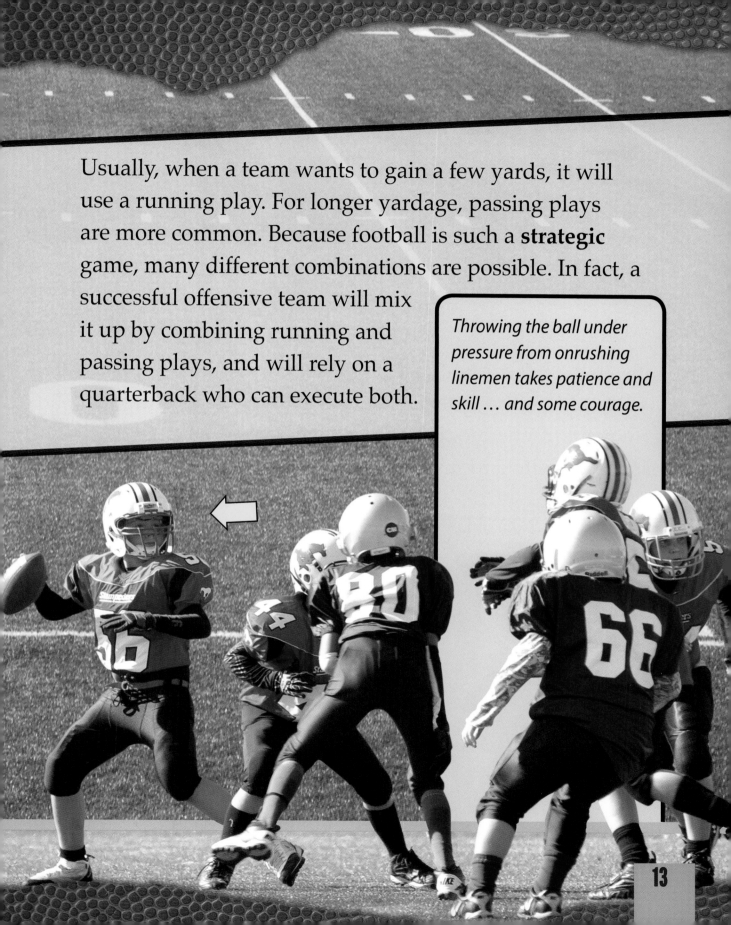

Usually, when a team wants to gain a few yards, it will use a running play. For longer yardage, passing plays are more common. Because football is such a **strategic** game, many different combinations are possible. In fact, a successful offensive team will mix it up by combining running and passing plays, and will rely on a quarterback who can execute both.

Throwing the ball under pressure from onrushing linemen takes patience and skill … and some courage.

ROLLOUT

Many times the quarterback himself will run with the ball. One type of planned play is the rollout. In this play, the quarterback takes the snap from the center and runs, or rolls, to the left or right, following the offensive linemen who block for him. The quarterback may continue to run to gain yards, or, before crossing the line of scrimmage, he can pass forward to a receiver or back to a running back.

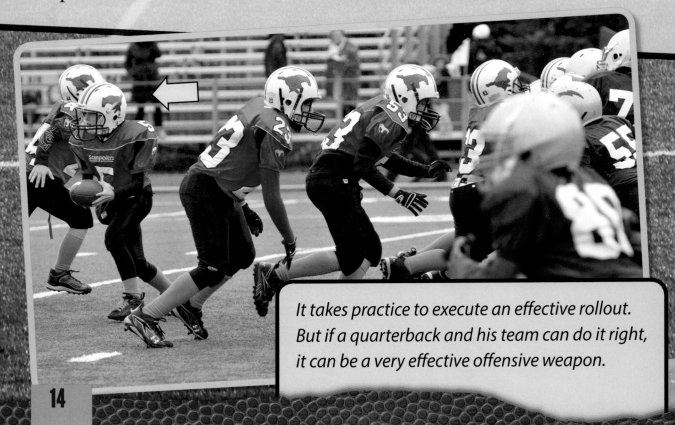

It takes practice to execute an effective rollout. But if a quarterback and his team can do it right, it can be a very effective offensive weapon.

Running quarterbacks—those who intentionally run for yards—are a lot more common in college football than in the pro game. Many college offenses are specifically designed to maximize the talents of a quarterback who can rush. But in the pros, quarterbacks are more likely to drop back into the pocket of space behind the line of scrimmage, where they can be protected by linemen.

Sometimes when a planned play does not work, the quarterback needs to run the ball on his own to try to gain yards. Many coaches do not like rollout plays because they expose the quarterback in the open field and put him in danger of being injured by a **tackle**.

When a play does not go according to plan, the quarterback takes off and looks for room to run. Of course, the defensive players try to tackle him before he can gain yards.

HAND OFF

On a running play, the quarterback takes the snap and spins to hand the ball to one of his running backs. This play needs to be practiced carefully so that both players have their timing just right. Any confusion may lead to a fumble.

A well-executed hand off gives the running back time and space to make his move. He will often look for a hole in the defensive line created by good blocks from teammates.

Once the quarterback hands the ball to the running back, he may help the offensive linemen block defenders to make room for the run. He can also fake a run himself to try to convince the defenders that he still has the ball.

The running back looks as if he has taken the ball and is heading upfield with it … but the quarterback really has it, and the fake hand off has worked once again!

PASSING SKILLS

One of the most important skills a quarterback needs is to be able to throw the ball to a receiver. But simply making a throw is only part of it. A quarterback needs to be able to avoid rushing defensive players who are trying to tackle him as well as figure out how to keep his pass out of the hands of defensive backs who are trying to intercept it.

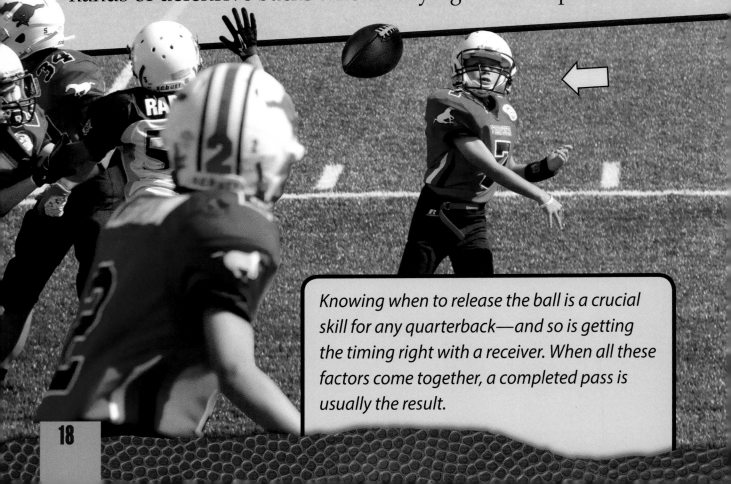

Knowing when to release the ball is a crucial skill for any quarterback—and so is getting the timing right with a receiver. When all these factors come together, a completed pass is usually the result.

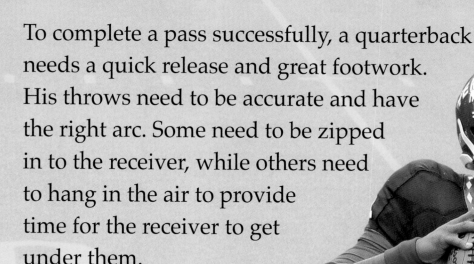

To complete a pass successfully, a quarterback needs a quick release and great footwork. His throws need to be accurate and have the right arc. Some need to be zipped in to the receiver, while others need to hang in the air to provide time for the receiver to get under them.

Quarterbacks are often judged by their completion rate—the number of passes they complete per number of passes attempted. Here, Temple University quarterback P. J. Walker steps up to throw downfield in a college game in 2013.

THE TYPES OF PASSES

To be a successful passing quarterback, you need to keep the defense guessing about the kinds of passes you are going to throw. On an offensive play, some receivers may run short routes, while others may go long. Some short passes may be part of a set offensive play, while others are delivered on the run while escaping defenders.

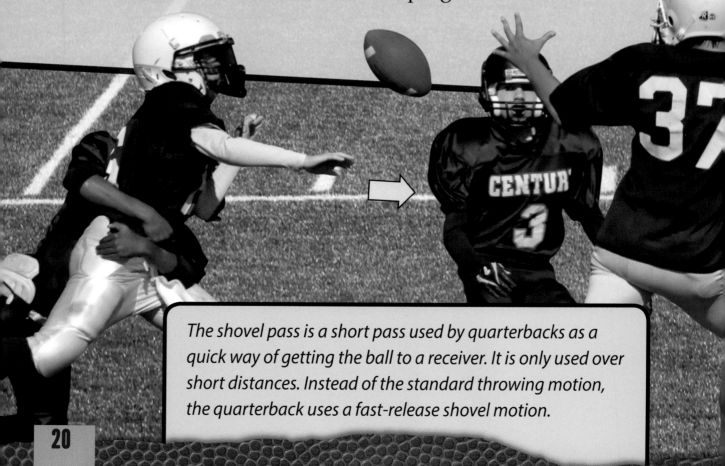

The shovel pass is a short pass used by quarterbacks as a quick way of getting the ball to a receiver. It is only used over short distances. Instead of the standard throwing motion, the quarterback uses a fast-release shovel motion.

It's the same for long passes. Some plays may call for a quarterback to drop straight back after taking the snap and, with a bit of extra time provided by the defensive line, aim for a receiver way downfield. Throwing a long pass is a high-risk play. It is difficult to throw that far and have the receiver catch the ball, but when it works, the receiver often scores a touchdown.

Other long passes have to be delivered while scrambling—and it's not easy to throw long while on the run!

THE PERFECT SPIRAL

The best way for a quarterback to throw accurately is to throw a spiral—a ball that spins as it flies through the air. With lots of practice, the quarterback can learn how to put just the right **rotation** on the ball. This helps it cut through the air rapidly and in a nice straight line.

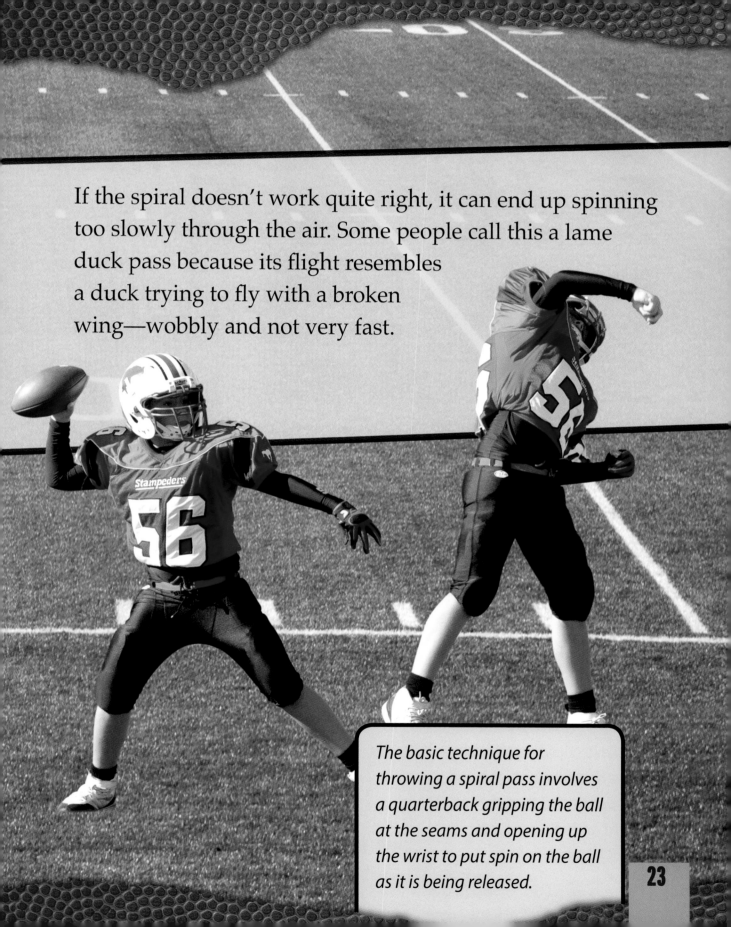

If the spiral doesn't work quite right, it can end up spinning too slowly through the air. Some people call this a lame duck pass because its flight resembles a duck trying to fly with a broken wing—wobbly and not very fast.

The basic technique for throwing a spiral pass involves a quarterback gripping the ball at the seams and opening up the wrist to put spin on the ball as it is being released.

THE ROLE OF A COACH

A good coach is crucial to any quarterback's development. Because of the important role a quarterback plays in the game, many of them end up becoming coaches when they retire from playing. An experienced coach can provide both **technical** advice on how to play the position and, just as important, guidance on how to lead a team and read opposing defenses.

On the sidelines, quarterbacks need to take in complicated instructions from the coaches and turn them into action on the field.

Coaches help quarterbacks in both practice sessions and games. It is very common to see coaches and quarterbacks talking to one another on the sidelines during a game. Coaches know that by passing on advice to the quarterback, they are really giving their ideas to the entire offense. Some specialized coaches work to train and advise only quarterbacks.

Coaches call offensive and defensive plays from the sidelines. Because of the crowd noise and general confusion on the field, they often use hand signals to get their message across.

THE BEST QUARTERBACKS

There have been hundreds of great quarterbacks, and football fans love to debate about who the best all-time players in this position have been. Old-school quarterbacks like Johnny Unitas, Bart Starr, and Fran Tarkenton set an example for many to follow in the 1950s, '60s, and '70s.

Aaron Rodgers (left) of the Green Bay Packers led the Packers to a win in the Super Bowl in 2010.

Tom Brady (right) has led the New England Patriots to the Super Bowl five times and won three times.

One great quarterback, Joe Montana of the San Francisco 49ers and the Kansas City Chiefs was called the Comeback Kid. He was famous for rallying his team back from almost-certain defeat in the final few minutes of games, which he did thirty-one times in his career.

In the modern game, there have also been many great quarterbacks. These include Brett Favre, John Elway, Troy Aikman, and Dan Marino.

Peyton Manning was the quarterback for the Indianapolis Colts from 1998 to 2011, winning one Super Bowl. Being a great quarterback must run in the family since his dad, Archie, was also a superstar … and so is his brother Eli!

BE A GOOD SPORT

Many people consider football to be a rough sport. There is a lot of contact between players. Good sportsmanship means putting forth your best effort in both games and practice, following the rules, and demonstrating fair play by respecting the decisions of your coaches and the officials.

Good sportsmanship is built on respect for your opponents.

As well, it is very important to treat **opponents** with respect—and in cases in which your opponents are not behaving respectfully, remembering not to retaliate verbally or physically. Staying in control is key in a physical sport like football. Even when the play gets tough, true champions keep their cool!

Football is a tough, physical sport. Nevertheless, good sportsmanship is encouraged at all levels of play. If players don't follow football etiquette there is greater risk of injury. For the most part football's rules of etiquette involve showing respect for teammates, coaches, and opponents.

GLOSSARY

blockers (BLAH-kurs) Players who are trying to stop the other team's players.

defense (DEE-fents) A group of players trying to stop points from being scored by the other team.

field goal (FEELD GOHL) A play in which the ball is kicked through the uprights of the goalpost.

formation (for-MAY-shun) The way the players are arranged on the field.

fumble (FUM-bul) To drop the ball.

line of scrimmage (LYN UV SKRIH-mij) The invisible line where the ball was last down and where the next play starts.

offense (O-fents) A group of players trying to score points for their team.

opponents (uh-POH-nents) The people or team you are competing against in a game.

rotation (roh-TAY-shun) The way a football turns as it moves through the air.

stance (STANS) A way of standing.

strategic (struh-TEE-jik) A type of clever plan.

tackle (TA-kul) To knock or throw another player to the ground.

technical (TEK-nuh-kul) Related to special knowledge.

FOR MORE INFORMATION

FURTHER READING

Gifford, Clive. *Football*. Sporting Skills. New York: Cavendish Square, 2010.

Mahaney, Ian F. *The Math of Football*. Sports Math. New York: PowerKids Press, 2012.

Stewart, Mark. *Football*. The Ultimate 10: Sports. New York: Gareth Stevens, 2009.

WEBSITES

Due to the changing nature of Internet links, PowerKids Press has developed an online list of websites related to the subject of this book. This site is updated regularly. Please use this link to access the list:

www.powerkidslinks.com/fbs/quar/

INDEX